*Changes*

*In the year and a half since he had died, Margaret thought of her father less and less. Before, he had been like his real self hovering over her, making her remember him every single day; now he was just a small shadow that followed her. All of a sudden she would look to the side or behind her and catch a glimpse of him. When this happened, her throat swelled up. She would feel the tears before they came to the surface. But she was crying for him less and less these days. Ms. Dell had said that was a good sign. Margaret disagreed. It was just a sign that there were other things in her life to cry about . . .*

"What works best here is the slice-of-life portrait of Margaret and Maizon's friendship: close, sometimes uneasy or prickly, but ultimately affirming."

—*The Bulletin of the Center for Children's Books*

## ALSO BY JACQUELINE WOODSON

*After Tupac and D Foster*

*Behind You*

*Beneath a Meth Moon*

*Brown Girl Dreaming*

*The Dear One*

*Feathers*

*From the Notebooks of Melanin Sun*

*The House You Pass on the Way*

*Hush*

*I Hadn't Meant to Tell You This*

*If You Come Softly*

*Last Summer with Maizon*

*Lena*

*Locomotion*

*Maizon at Blue Hill*

*Miracle's Boys*

*Peace, Locomotion*

# Between Madison and Palmetto

JACQUELINE WOODSON

PUFFIN BOOKS

PUFFIN BOOKS
An imprint of Penguin Random House LLC
375 Hudson Street
New York, New York 10014

First published in the United States of America by Delacorte Press, 1993
Published by G. P. Putnam's Sons, a division of Penguin Putnam Books for Young Readers, 2002
Published by Puffin Books, a division of Penguin Putnam Books for Young Readers, 2002

THE LIBRARY OF CONGRESS HAS CATALOGED THE G. P. PUTNAM'S SONS EDITION AS FOLLOWS:
Woodson, Jacqueline.
Between Madison & Palmetto / Jacqueline Woodson.—1st G. P. Putnam's Sons ed.
p. cm.
Sequel to: Maison at Blue Hill.
Summary: When Margaret's best friend Maizon returns from boarding school and
joins her in the eighth grade, they try to resume their friendship while dealing with
personal problems and watching their Brooklyn neighborhood undergo changes.
[1. Friendship—Fiction. 2. African Americans—Fiction.
3. Brooklyn (New York, N.Y.)—Fiction.]
I. Title: Between Madison and Palmetto. II. Title.
PZ7.W868 Be 2002 [Fic]—dc20    2001041741

Puffin Books ISBN 978-0-698-11958-1

Printed in the United States of America

14  16  18  20  19  17  15

For my family

# 1

Rain came the day after Christmas—hard, cold drops that lasted into the night, tapering to a drizzle by next morning—only to start up a crazy torrent again toward the end of the day.

By New Year's Eve, the rain had turned to snow. It started out melting the moment it hit the ground, then little by little began to stick, first in patches, then building into heavy white puffs of hills up and down Madison Street.

Margaret stared out of Ms. Dell's window. Behind her, the New Year's party was in full blast. She must have suffered through a hundred Happy New Year kisses. Now it was a little after midnight.

"May old acquaintance be forgot!" Maizon sang at the top of her lungs, coming up behind Margaret and handing her a glass of sparkling cider. Maizon raised her own glass into the air.

"And never brought to Rome," Margaret chimed in. They clinked glasses, then gulped the cider and giggled.

They had dressed alike for the party. Margaret pulled at the collar of the black crushed-velvet dress and picked some lint from the black tights she and Maizon had bought to go with the dresses.

"I want to go upstairs and put on something more comfortable," Margaret said. She had lived five floors up from Ms. Dell for a long time now, but still it was hard to get used to the idea of climbing all those stairs and traipsing back down again for the sake of an outfit.

"No way, José," Maizon said. "Then I'll have to go home and change." She lived down the street from Margaret in one of the most beautiful brownstones on the block. "I'm not about to go all the way home. Not with the party going strong."

Before the party, Margaret's baby broher, Li'l Jay, had cried when he saw Maizon's and Margaret's outfits. "This!"

he insisted, yanking his black sweatsuit from the dresser drawer. Margaret's mother had scowled at the outfit but gave Li'l Jay his way.

"Somebody die?" Ms. Dell teased as she walked past the trio with a plate of tiny sandwiches. Dressed in a black skirt and jacket with a string of pearls around her neck, she looked younger than fifty.

"What's your prediction, Ms. Dell?" Maizon asked, moving in front of her.

"Prediction for what?" Ms. Dell said too innocently, raising her eyebrows. Ms. Dell was clairvoyant. Although both Margaret and Maizon had coveted her gift of sight, they had discovered that Ms. Dell had passed her gift on to Li'l Jay. Each time the phone rang, Li'l Jay would shout out the name of the person on the other end before anyone answered it. He could tell who was walking up the block without looking out the window. Li'l Jay knew what Margaret was doing even when they were in different parts of the house. It was starting to drive her a little crazy.

"The future," Maizon said. "What's going to happen this year? Is everybody going to get rich?"

"We already are rich. Rich in family and friends."

Ms. Dell took a sandwich from the tray and stuffed it into Maizon's mouth. Margaret giggled, covering her mouth with her hand.

"I predict this year will have three hundred and sixty-five days in it." Ms. Dell laughed, pushing Maizon out of the way.

"Some things never change," Maizon said, after Ms. Dell had gone. She eyed Li'l Jay. "What a waste. A perfectly good gift of clairvoyance and he gets it."

Li'l Jay laughed and hugged Maizon's leg.

"This kid barely talks. What good is being clairvoyant if you can't communicate?"

"He talks enough," Margaret said. "He's discovered the art of tattling on me in five words or less."

"Not me." Li'l Jay giggled.

"Yes you, li'l brother."

"Happy Year!!" Li'l Jay yelled.

Margaret's mother walked in with Hattie, Ms. Dell's daughter.

"Hi, Mama," Margaret yelled, kissing her on the cheek.

"Hi, Mrs. Tory," Maizon said. She nodded to Hattie, who winked at both of them.

Last summer Hattie had decided to go back to school to study nursing. Now, at twenty-one, she was already working at a hospital three days a week as part of her training. Margaret couldn't wait until the day when she walked into a doctor's office and it was Hattie who pressed the tongue depressor down her throat. Hattie with her soft warm hands and sad brown eyes. A long time ago, when Hattie was a lot younger, her baby died at birth. Margaret figured this was the reason Hattie was back in school now, learning how to save other people's lives.

"We're finally going to have original art in the house," Hattie said.

Mrs. Tory hammered a nail into the wall above the kitchen table. "I think this is a nice spot."

"Perfect," Hattie said.

"Perfect for what?" Maizon asked, moving closer to the table.

Mrs. Tory took a picture from brown wrapping. It was a small painting, about the size of a notebook.

"That's your painting, Mama," Margaret said, moving closer to get a better look. The painting was what Mama had called an abstract. There were lots of oranges and reds and blues moving over the canvas in a way that made Margaret think of a rainbow melting into the night. When she looked closer, she could read the writing at the corner. *Rainbow Melting*, it said in thin black letters. Beside the title Mrs. Tory had signed her name: *Linda Vicky Tory*.

"You named it what I told you it reminded me of," Margaret whispered. Mrs. Tory smiled and nodded. She had braided her hair and woven the braids into a crown around her head. The style made her look younger, more lively. *She looks so beautiful tonight*, Margaret thought, reaching out and hugging her. "Happy New Year, Mama."

Behind them, Margaret could hear Maizon humming "Auld Lang Syne" off-key, the way they both sang and hummed.

"Hug me," Li'l Jay demanded. Mama reached down and joined him in the circle.

"Real art," Hattie was saying. "Ump. Ump. Ump."

"This is getting corny," Maizon said. "I'm going to find my grandma."

# 2

Maizon found Grandma sitting on the couch talking to Bo. *What could they have to talk about?* Maizon thought. Bo had been at the same elementary school with her and Margaret. Then, in sixth grade, Maizon had gone off to Blue Hill, a boarding school where she had gotten a scholarship. She only stayed a few months, but while she was gone, Bo and Margaret hung out together a lot. Maizon knew Margaret had a crush the size of the hole in the ozone layer on Bo, but when Maizon asked her about it, Margaret made believe she couldn't care less. Now she and Margaret were both in the seventh grade at Pace Academy, a private school. Since Bo still lived in the neighborhood, they'd ended up hanging with him more than they ever had before.

"Yo, Bo," Maizon said, taking a seat beside her grandmother on the couch.

"Hey, Maiz." Bo smiled. "Happy New Year."

"Happy New Year," Maizon said. She could definitely understand what Margaret saw in Bo. There was a time when even she had thought he was cute. He had smooth dark skin and the high cheekbones that made girls act silly whenever he smiled. But she had grown out of the giggly phase. When she and Bo talked now, it was about serious stuff like the Knicks' coach or Magic Johnson's HIV diagnosis or the changes in the neighborhood. She didn't get butterflies anymore like she had once a long time ago. It was as if she had grown used to Bo now and could see him as he was—a possible friend, an equal. Somebody who had some smart things to say and who liked a good slam-dunk every now and then. Once, she and Bo had even gone one-on-one on the basketball court. Bo creamed her. But afterward he spent a good hour showing her how to do lay-ups and hook shots. While they were playing, a crowd of girls had started milling around the court. Maizon knew it wasn't because they were interested in basketball—they were interested in Bo. One girl even stopped Maizon on her way out of the park. "How do you get him to pay attention to you like that?" the girl had asked. "He's so cute." Maizon looked at the girl for a moment. She was about Maizon's age but she was wearing lipstick and eyeliner and had about eight holes pierced into one ear. Then Maizon shrugged. "I don't do anything special. I'm just—just myself." The girl looked puzzled. Maizon felt a little sorry for her.

Now Bo pulled his chair closer to the couch and, excusing himself, leaned over Grandma to speak to Maizon. The music was loud. Behind them, people were dancing. Every now and then someone blew into a noisemaker and shouted, "Happy New Year!"

"I was just telling your grandma about Baldwin Prep."

Grandma smiled, rubbing Maizon's leg. "It sounds like a good school."

Maizon nodded. She and Margaret had walked twelve blocks out of their way more than once to pass Baldwin Prep—the all-black, all-boy school Bo was attending now.

Baldwin Prep was a school for kids who hadn't done well academically in the regular school system. SELF-ESTEEM, SELF-AWARENESS, SELF-LOVE was engraved in block letters on the front of the school building. It was the first all-black boys' school in the city.

"I can't believe there could be this many fine brothers in one place," Maizon had said as she and Margaret walked slowly past the high fence enclosing the school-yard. It had been a day when Pace Academy students were dismissed early because of parent-teacher conferences. Margaret and Maizon had bolted off the school bus and made it to Baldwin Prep just as lunch was ending. "Bummer," Maizon said, as she and Margaret watched the backs of the dozens of boys heading back into the red-brick building. "We missed them."

"We squashed Stuyvesant seventy-eight to thirty-six right before Christmas." Bo smiled now, looking off as though he were remembering the game. "Felt a little sorry for them," he said, shaking his head. "Nobody should lose that badly."

Grandma smiled, but Maizon threw her head back and laughed. She could almost picture Baldwin Prep, looking like the Harlem Globetrotters—the basketball team so good, they're not even allowed to play professionally—running circles around Stuyvesant.

Grandma leaned over to kiss Maizon, then stood up slowly. "Think I'm going to head home, Maizon. Are you spending the night at Margaret's?"

"Can I?"

Grandma nodded. "If it's okay with Mrs. Tory. I'll check with her on my way out."

"Be careful on the ice, Grandma."

"Good night, Bo. Nice talking to you."

"You, too, Mrs. Singh."

Maizon scooted over to Grandma's place on the couch.

"I have a question, Maiz . . ." Bo began.

"Shoot."

"If your grandma is your mom's mother, how come you two have the same last name?"

"After my mama died and my dad left, Grandma officially adopted me. I was a baby."

Bo shrugged. "Makes sense to me. Another question."

"Get them answered while you can."

"What's it like to grow up without a pops? I mean, I

think about it because I know a lot of kids who don't have a dad. But I can't picture what it would be like to not have my dad in the picture. There'd be an empty chair in the kitchen. My parents' bedroom would always seem half empty. And forget about my life. It would just seem like I was floating from one place to another. I mean, my dad is always there for me. We shoot hoops together, take walks, see movies, talk about girls . . ." Bo shook his head. "I don't even like to think about what it would be like without him."

Maizon thought for a moment. "I don't have any of that stuff to compare it to. He was never in the picture. You can't miss something that was never there, right?"

"What was never there?" Margaret asked, walking up and taking a place beside Maizon on the couch. They linked arms.

"My father," Maizon said, and saw how Margaret's face seemed to drop, a microslice of an inch that only a close friend would notice. It had been a year and a half since Margaret's father died of a heart attack. Maizon realized how the emptiness Bo talked about seemed to encircle Margaret's life, even though Margaret tried to hide it.

There was a sadness about her that had never been there before.

They were all silent for an awkward moment.

Impulsively, Maizon leaned over and kissed Margaret on the cheek. She wanted to be Margaret's closest friend in the world. She wanted Margaret to belong only to her. Something kept gnawing at her, though, telling her this might not happen. Still, she didn't stop hoping.

"So what's up at Pace?" Bo asked, breaking the silence.

"Lotsa lotsa things. I wrote a play, so of course Margaret is directing."

"And Caroline is starring," Margaret added.

Bo raised an eyebrow. "That white girl from Palmetto Street?"

They nodded.

Bo rolled his eyes.

"What do you have against her?" Maizon asked.

Bo raised both hands and shrugged. "Same thing I have against all of them."

"That's racist, Bo—" Margaret began.

"Gimme a break, Margaret. You mean to tell me you don't see what's happening to this neighborhood?"

Margaret leaned back against the couch. "Yeah, I see. New buildings going up. The street cleaner coming around more. What's wrong with that? We need the streets cleaned."

"Ah Margaret, c'mon. It's because of white people"—Bo looked over at Maizon—"like your friend Caroline."

"Well, what has she personally done to you?" Maizon asked.

"Man!" Bo leaned forward, as though he could make them understand by moving closer. "I'm almost six feet tall."

Maizon raised her eyebrows. "Yeah?"

"I'm black."

Margaret smiled. "No kidding?"

"I'm a man."

"A teenager," Maizon corrected. "You're thirteen."

Bo shook his head. "Whatever. It doesn't matter. What matters is you get me on a dark street with your Caroline or your Caroline's mom, and if they don't run like Pete to cross the street, my name's not Bo Douglas."

Margaret and Maizon were silent.

"If it wasn't for Baldwin Prep teaching me that it's okay to walk through this world a black male," Bo continued, "I'd probably be feeling kind of low."

"We don't get taught that stuff and we feel okay," Margaret said.

"Just okay?" Bo smirked. "Who wants to feel *okay*? I want to feel *great* about who I am."

"Well, there should be a school for black girls like that. How come boys get everything?" Maizon said. She couldn't help thinking about Blue Hill and all the white girls there. There had only been four other black students and she had been so lonely for Madison Street, for the dark faces of her friends and grandmother. She hadn't felt as sure of herself at Blue Hill as she felt on Madison Street. She looked at Bo. "But I know what you're saying."

"Me too," Margaret said. "But what does that have to do with the construction?"

Bo looked as if he were about to say something, then stopped. After a moment, he said, "You'll see." He looked around at the crowded party. In the corner of the living room Hattie, her back to the wall, laughed into the face of her current boyfriend. Ms. Dell sat across the room, rocking a sleeping Li'l Jay on her lap while she talked to a woman in a green Sunday hat. A bluesy song was playing softly now.

"We'll all see," Bo said.

# 3

"Years pass," Ms. Dell said slowly. It had been a week since the New Year's party, and still confetti littered the corners of the kitchen and living room. Ms. Dell sat opposite Margaret at the huge kitchen table. Behind her, Hattie was busy at the stove, warming up soup for their lunch. In a few minutes Hattie, looking older than twenty-one in Ms. Dell's apron, would be setting a steaming bowl of it in front of Margaret, warming up every single part of her against the chill. Outside, snow had laid a thick white cape over every inch of Madison Street. Li'l Jay napped in the bedroom off of the kitchen—Hattie's room. "Here it is more than a year since Maizon went away and came back from that boarding school."

Hattie looked over her shoulder at Margaret. "You two are growing up before everybody's eyes. Where is Maizon, anyway?"

Margaret shrugged. "I don't know and I don't care." She hadn't seen much of Maizon since the New Year's party. Tomorrow would be the first day of school since Christmas break. Maybe she'd see Maizon on the bus. The smell of Hattie's spicy chicken soup filled the kitchen. Margaret couldn't believe how hungry she was.

"Uh-oh," Hattie said under her breath.

"She's probably with Caroline or something."

"How come Caroline didn't come to the party?" Ms. Dell asked.

"They were away visiting her grandparents in Vermont. I guess she's back now and Maizon's being buddy-buddy with her."

Hattie smiled. "Sounds like a little bit of jealousy to me."

"I don't care about it. She can hang out with whoever she wants." Margaret cut her eyes at Hattie. Hunger made her crabby.

"Sometimes," Ms. Dell continued, "it seems as though not a moment has moved, but then you look up and you're already old or you already have a houseful of kids or you look down and see your feet are miles and miles away from the rest of you—and you realize you've grown up."

Without thinking, Margaret looked down. Already her breasts had begun to build tiny mountains on her chest. Mama had bought her three bras, each one a little bit stretchier than the last. She smoothed her hands over her chest. The bulky sweaters she wore almost hid this growing she had absolutely no control over. But her jeans didn't hide the extra meat rounding out her behind and thighs. Hattie laughed. Margaret raised her head slowly, knowing already that Hattie would be looking at her and smiling. This wasn't the first time she had been caught checking out this new unfamiliar body of hers. Margaret felt her face growing hot.

"You'll get used to it, Margaret," Hattie said, setting a bowl of soup down in front of her.

"I'd rather it just went away."

"But it doesn't—" Hattie began.

"I know, Hattie," Margaret said, cutting her off. "That

doesn't make me stop wishing." She took a spoonful of soup before continuing. "Every morning I wake up, it seems everything is bigger than it was the day before. I hate all this growing!"

"So many girls wish they had breasts." Ms. Dell laughed. "Girls walking around all flat chested, stuffing their bras with tissue, doing exercises and praying. You should count yourself lucky."

"How fat am I gonna get?"

"It's not fat," Hattie said softly, touching Margaret's forehead. "It's just growing." She sat down in the chair closest to Margaret, tore a piece of the warm bread Ms. Dell had baked, and dipped it into her soup. "When I was little, I used to be so flat chested, I didn't even want to go outside. Remember, Mama?"

Ms. Dell nodded, smiling. "How could I forget that little girl standing at the screen door looking sad and me not knowing the reason?"

"Those girls down south," Hattie continued, "seemed to be stacked by the time they were ten. They had two years on you, Margaret. But when we moved up here to

20

New York, I seemed to be caught up with everybody. Then it was safe to go outside again."

Hattie laughed. "Eat your soup."

Margaret smiled, taking a big spoonful. Leave it to Ms. Dell and Hattie to make her feel okay about herself.

"What time's your mama home, tonight?" Ms. Dell asked.

"She said around eight. There's a meeting today. Some people might want her to do some illustrations for a magazine. If they do, she said they're going to pay her good money."

A few months after her father died, Margaret's mother started working for an architectural firm while she took drawing classes at City College at night. Now she had a new job, designing everything from company manuals to Christmas-party matchbooks.

Ms. Dell shook her head proudly and turned to get what must have been the hundredth look at the picture Mrs. Tory had given them New Year's Eve. "Every one of you Torys has a gift," she said slowly. "Even your father, God rest his soul."

"God rest it," Margaret and Hattie echoed.

In the year and a half since he had died, Margaret thought of her father less and less. Before, he had been like his real self hovering over her, making her remember him every single day; now he was just a small shadow that followed her. All of a sudden she would look to the side or behind her and catch a glimpse of him. When this happened, her throat swelled up. She would feel the tears before they came to the surface. But she was crying for him less and less these days. Ms. Dell had said that was a good sign. Margaret disagreed. It was just a sign that there were other things in her life to cry about. There was the empty apartment that greeted her when she ran in from school some days, hoping her mother would be there, having forgotten that Mama would be at work. There was Li'l Jay, growing tall and talking more and more, Li'l Jay with his gift of clairvoyance like Ms. Dell's. But most of all, Margaret knew, behind all the other things to cry about, there was Maizon. The old Maizon and the new one. The one that had gone off to Blue Hill and come home different. The Maizon who hardly ever called up to her window anymore, who walked to the pizzeria with Caroline Berg, who sat on the school bus with her only when Caroline was absent or being driven to Pace Academy by her dad.

*It's not fair*, Margaret thought. Maizon hadn't even liked Caroline in the beginning. It was Margaret who wanted them all to be friends. Maizon had thought Caroline would be like all the white girls at Blue Hill. Margaret closed her eyes and remembered climbing on the Pace Academy bus in front of Maizon for the first time.

"A school bus and everything," Margaret said excitedly. "This is going to be great."

But Maizon had been solemn and reluctant. She had told Margaret she was sick and tired of going from school to school and just wanted to find a place where she belonged.

"You'll belong here," Margaret promised, pulling Maizon into the seat beside her.

Caroline was sitting in front of them, alone, staring out of the window. Her hair hung down over the back of the seat and reminded Margaret of strawberries, dark and red. But it wasn't really red. It was more blond with strips of brown running faintly through it.

"Hi," Margaret said.

Caroline turned and Margaret caught the frown racing across Maizon's face and knew Maizon had recognized Caroline from the window on Palmetto Street.

"Hey!" Caroline smiled. Her eyes were just a little darker than her hair and her smile seemed to light them up. *It's a nice face*, Margaret thought. *It's honest*. Margaret remembered the sad-looking girl waving to them from the window. When Caroline smiled, she wasn't that person anymore.

"Hey yourself," Maizon said.

Those first days at Pace Academy had been great. The teachers seemed to treat every student as though they were the only student. Although Margaret and Maizon only had a few classes together, they had the same lunch period and had spent the early days catching up on everything going on during that time. But as it turned out, Maizon and Caroline had practically every class together and Margaret watched from the sidelines as they grew closer and closer. Soon, all Maizon was talking about at lunch was Caroline. Pace Academy didn't seem so perfect anymore. It was just another school with a bunch of smart kids. And Margaret felt more alone than she ever had before.

"Years pass," Ms. Dell said again, looking over at Margaret.

Margaret took another sip of chicken soup.

"Years pass," Li'l Jay echoed, walking sleepily into the kitchen. "I want soup."

# 4

Maizon made her way slowly up Palmetto Street, past the empty plots where cranes and cement mixers sat silently waiting for Monday when they'd start up again. Cranes and cement mixers working five days a week to change this neighborhood into something it hadn't been before.

"Life," Ms. Dell had said to Maizon and Margaret the summer before Maizon left for Blue Hill, "moves us through all the time changes. All kinds of changes. And we're made so that we roll and move with it. Sometimes somebody gets stuck in the present and the rolling stops — but the changing doesn't."

It seemed now everyone was rolling nervously, waiting for the next change to shiver, like a late winter wind, through the neighborhood. Everyone, Ms. Dell and Hattie and Mrs. Tory, waited anxiously. They were afraid of these changes. If the fixing continued and the neighborhood improved, richer people would begin to move in, the way Caroline's family and other families had moved onto Palmetto Street. Ms. Dell and Mrs. Tory rented their apartments. They were afraid the rents would increase because people moving in had more money to pay. If the rent increased, they'd have to move. Maizon had heard Ms. Dell talking to Grandma about it. Grandma owned the house she and Maizon lived in. People had tried to buy it, offering her lots of money, even showing her the cash. But Grandma had held fast. In the end, she had forced the men from her house, daring them to ever come back again.

"They think black people go crazy for money," Grandma had said sadly, shaking her head. "This house is ours, Maizon. That's the way it will always be."

But now, as she turned the corner, heading to Caroline's, bending her head against the cold rush of wind,

Maizon wasn't so sure about "always." It contradicted Ms. Dell's statement about change. Everything contradicted everything. Even her friendship with Caroline was a contradiction. Bo flashed across her mind. *You get me on a dark street with your Caroline or your Caroline's mom, and if they don't run like Pete to cross the street, my name's not Bo Douglas.* Maybe he was right too.

At the corner, Maizon stopped. Woodbine Street. She looked up at the black-and-white street sign. Woodbine used to be between Madison and Palmetto. A long time ago there had been a whole block of houses where there was nothing now. *A whole block just disappearing*, Maizon thought to herself. *A whole neighborhood*. Years ago, Ms. Dell had told them, Woodbine had fallen victim to fire after fire. Soon there were only a few houses, scattered up and down the block. Now even those were gone and the big, empty lot that once had been the homes of families, escaped the notice of a lot of people. Maizon couldn't remember the last time she had thought about the block that used to be between Madison and Palmetto. *Where there once was, there isn't now.* The line was from a poem someone had written at Blue Hill. Maizon couldn't remember the girl's name. They hadn't been friends. The title of the poem was "Disappearance." The class had taken the poem apart line by line while the author sat silently, occasionally nodding but not offering up any of her own reasons for writing it. Only now, standing on the corner, could Maizon add this to her ideas of what the girl had been trying to say.

> Into the trailing daybreak air,
> I ride aloft a memory there
> Against the winding cry of this plow
> Where there once was, there isn't now.

Maybe Bo had been right when he'd said, "We'll all see." Maybe everyone in the neighborhood was on the edge of riding aloft a memory of the old Madison. In the years to come, Maizon wondered, would Madison Street drop off the face of the earth the way Woodbine had?

She rang Caroline's buzzer and waited. The high-rise apartment building always smelled so new and clean. No smell of chicken frying in an apartment on the first floor. No peas and onions bubbling in a pot on the second.

There was something almost too sterile about this new building. As she made her way up the marble staircase to Caroline's third-floor apartment, Maizon wondered if this building would always smell so new.

On the day of Margaret's father's funeral, she and Margaret had gone outside, away from the Torys' crowded apartment.

"Ms. Dell says rich people are going to move into those new buildings," Maizon had said. They had worn identical black dresses that day. In the July heat the dresses clung to their skin.

They had always dressed alike back then. Now— Maizon sighed—they hardly ever wore the same clothes anymore. And rich people had moved into this building. Caroline's father was a college professor. Her mother wrote for magazines.

Maizon had been so deep in thought, she had forgotten why she was coming over until Caroline opened the door and stared at her. "Check this out!" Maizon said, opening her coat and running her hands over her new outfit. The look Caroline gave her reminded her of the time she had gone to Margaret's house dressed exactly like a fashion model she had seen in a magazine. *"Your grandmother's going to skin you alive when she finds out you left the house looking like that,"* Margaret had said when Maizon walked into her house wearing big gold hooped earrings and eyeliner. Margaret had been right, Maizon realized days later. The outfit had been a little bit ridiculous. But this one—now, this one was hot!

Caroline leaned against the door and smiled, dimples cutting deep into the sides of her face. Seeing her standing there, smiling, Maizon was sorry for how mean she had been the first time she saw Caroline: "Who's she?" Maizon had asked Margaret, glaring at the pale girl with her face pressed against the window, staring down at them. Maizon had just returned from Blue Hill. "I don't know," Margaret had answered. "She just moved in. I can see her staring all the time from my window." Margaret had waved, and Caroline waved back.

When they first met, last January, Maizon had not even said hello to Caroline on the school bus.

"Old Sunshine Face," she had nicknamed Caroline. "Always so bright and cheery."

"I think she's nice," Margaret had said.

But somehow it had been Maizon who became tight with Caroline. Margaret seemed happier spending time with Ms. Dell and Hattie and, more and more, by herself. When Maizon had asked her what she did when she was alone, Margaret had grown defensive. "Things!" she said, angrily. "Mostly I sleep." Maizon had stopped asking after that. When she called and Margaret said she'd rather be alone, Maizon left her alone. She missed her, though.

*Things turn around and around*, Maizon thought as she smiled back at Caroline.

"Cool, huh?" she said, coming into the living room and peeling off the heavy coat her grandmother had made her wear on top of the new outfit. "I don't think a thirteen-year-old should dress in black no matter how in-style it is," Grandma had complained, even as she stitched the Lycra material into an outfit.

Caroline whistled. "That's really nice, Maizon. You look like Catwoman."

"It's called a cat suit. My grandma made it . . . reluctantly."

"She spoils you." Caroline laughed, hanging Maizon's coat in the huge closet at the end of the living room.

"I deserve it," Maizon said, surprised again by the way the material shimmered, as though it had been sprinkled with gold dust. She pranced back and forth in front of Caroline, stopping to admire herself in the mirrored wall opposite Caroline's living-room window. But Grandma was right, Maizon realized. The cat suit emphasized the fact that she didn't have a single curve. Although she was nearly as tall as Hattie now, close to five eight, she didn't have anything to show for it. And now that her hair had grown out, hanging almost to her shoulders, it looked like a wild bush unbraided. Maizon tugged at it. Grandma had been right . . . again. Her hair did look ridiculous just sticking out all over her head.

"What're you doing?" Caroline asked, coming to stand beside Maizon at the mirror.

"I'm braiding this mess up. Look at me. I'm a wreck!"

Maizon watched Caroline watching her. They looked so different standing next to each other: where Caroline was pale and blond and came only up to Maizon's shoulder, Maizon was tall, the color of coffee beans, with hair dark and thick as steel wool.

"I like it loose," Caroline said, shrugging.

"Looks dumb," Maizon said. "I look like a wild child."

"Wish I had hair like that," Caroline said.

"You'd really look like a wild child, Caroline. Imagine you with my hair."

Caroline tilted her head sideways, as though she were really imagining it. Then they both burst out laughing.

"Is Margaret coming?" Caroline asked.

Maizon finished French braiding her hair.

"She's probably hanging with Ms. Dell and Hattie, the people who live downstairs from her," Maizon said. She had walked right past Margaret's building on her way to Caroline's. Even though things had changed between them, she still felt guilty about it. She looked back at the mirror. "Maybe if I put tissue in my—"

"Forget it, Maizon." Caroline laughed. "You can't show up at school flat chested one day and completely developed the next."

"When I was at Blue Hill, some of the girls used to walk around the bathroom with hardly anything on. I hated that. It seemed like they were showing off or some-thing!"

Maizon looked away from the mirror. She had been

back over a year, and still there were things missing. It reminded her of Woodbine—that wide gap of space, sitting there, filling itself in with air.

"Isn't Margaret supposed to be directing us?" Caroline said now, cutting into Maizon's thoughts.

"Yes. . . ." Maizon said slowly.

"Well, we only have two months before production!" Caroline was fanning herself with her script now. Maizon had written the monologue Caroline was doing. It was about a girl who gets lost on her way home from school even though she is walking the same route she has walked a thousand times. A *Metaphor,* she called the piece, and decided she couldn't write it and act in it too—that would not only be unprofessional, it would be downright greedy. Pace Academy put on student productions every year and asked students to submit plays. Margaret had also submitted a play but it hadn't been picked. Maizon couldn't help feeling a tinge of satisfaction at this. She still hadn't gotten over the jealousy she'd felt when Margaret's poem won an all-city poetry contest.

"I'm going to give her a call," Caroline said, heading for the phone.

"No," Maizon said quickly. Caroline put the phone down and turned back toward Maizon. "I'll go get her." She slipped her coat over the outfit and headed back toward the three flights of stairs.

# 5

"Margaret sick," Li'l Jay said, looking up at Maizon from a pile of trucks in the center of the living-room floor.

"Shut up, Li'l Jay." Margaret emerged from the bathroom. "Hey, Maizon."

"Hey," Maizon said. "What's wrong? You don't look so well."

Margaret pressed her hand against her stomach. "Hattie's soup."

"She was crying," Li'l Jay said, dragging a truck across Maizon's feet.

"You okay?" Maizon felt her friend's head.

"I just threw up a little. I hate that feeling. But, yeah, I'm okay now. What's up?"

"Saturday rehearsal at Caroline's," Maizon said.

"Jeez! I forgot. I was so busy hanging with Hattie and Ms. Dell, it completely slipped my mind. I knew there was something I was supposed to be doing."

"I'm not sick," Li'l Jay said. "Just Margaret. I ate soup too."

Margaret eyed Li'l Jay. A long time ago she couldn't wait for him to start talking. Now she just wished he'd shut up.

Maizon raised an eyebrow. "You sure you're okay, Margaret?"

"Yes already!" Margaret said. "Can't a person get sick without the world stopping?"

"What's your problem? I just asked a question."

"And I just answered it. I ate soup. It made me sick. I threw up. Case closed."

Maizon shrugged and walked across the living room. Mrs. Tory had painted a new picture, from a photograph. In it Maizon and Margaret had their arms thrown across each other's shoulders. They were smiling out at somebody, looking away from the camera. Maizon couldn't remember who it was they had been smiling at.

"This is from the photograph Hattie took that summer before I went away," Maizon said.

Margaret came over and stood beside her. She took Maizon's hand in her own and nodded.

"That was the best summer, Margaret," Maizon said softly. "It was like everything was perfect. Look how happy we were."

Margaret stared at the painting a long time. Mama had painted it perfectly. The picture had been taken at the very beginning of the summer before Daddy got sick. Before Maizon heard that she'd been accepted at Blue Hill. It had seemed like the whole summer was stretched out in front of them; like someone had handed them their whole life on silver platters and said, "Go have a good time with this." But then, maybe a month after that picture was taken, Daddy got sick and it was like that same someone returned and snatched the platter back.

"Do you feel okay to go over to Caroline's?" Maizon asked, squeezing Margaret's hand.

Margaret nodded. Maizon was staring at her in a way that made it seem like her friend was looking right through her. She stared back at Maizon a moment, then dropped her gaze. They stood like that for a while, in front of the painting, until Maizon let go of her hand.

"Did you make yourself throw up, Margaret?" she whispered.

Margaret swallowed. She had never lied to Maizon. She couldn't look at her now, and stood there staring at the floor.

"Some people do that," Maizon said. "I was just—I was just wondering if you . . . you know, were you doing that too—because it's not good for you. It messes you up inside."

"That soup was fattening," Margaret said. "Hattie makes it too rich."

"But you're not even a little bit fat. You're perfect. I wish I looked like you."

"I am not," Margaret said. "I'm getting fat all over."

"Margaret!" Maizon grabbed her shoulders, making Margaret look up into her eyes. "You're perfect."

Margaret pulled away. "We should go," she said, walking over to the couch for her coat. "Put your shoes on, Li'l Jay. You're going down to Ms. Dell's."

"Dell's house. Dell's house!" Li'l Jay sang, pulling his shoe onto the wrong foot.

When Margaret looked over at Maizon, she was still standing there, her hands hanging at her sides, looking helpless. That wasn't like her.

"Do you do that a lot, Margaret?"

"I don't want to talk about it, Maizon. It doesn't matter, okay?"

"It *does* matter."

Margaret shoved Li'l Jay's shoes onto the right feet and lifted him off of the floor. "Get your jacket," she said. "Maybe Ms. Dell will take you outside."

Li'l Jay ran into his bedroom.

"Look, Maizon," Margaret said. "I only do it some-times and I still eat healthy stuff most of the time. I'm only going to do it until I feel good about my body, okay? Right now, I feel crappy."

"But you look good, Margaret!"

"But I don't like the way I look. That's what matters, Maizon. How I feel, all right? Not how you feel about how I look or how Ms. Dell or Hattie or Mama feels. How I feel."

Li'l Jay ran back into the living room, pulling his coat on.

Maizon shook her head, then hit the side of it as though she couldn't believe what she was hearing.

"When I was at Blue Hill, there were girls who wouldn't eat or they'd eat a whole lot and then go puke somewhere, and I was thinking, *Oh, man—don't you girls know that you're not even close to being fat?* I was thinking, *Wait till I get back to Brooklyn and tell Margaret about this—then we can dog them together and talk about how stupid it all is.* But here I am, and here you are doing exactly what those girls were doing, and it's like I'm right back there. You're the last person in the world I thought would be doing something like this, Margaret."

"Margaret sick. . . ." Li'l Jay whispered, his eyes widening.

Margaret pulled him close and hugged him. "No, I'm not, Li'l Jay," she said. But Li'l Jay began to cry. Margaret felt her stomach flutter and, looking up at Maizon, knew her friend was thinking the same thing. Because of his gift of clairvoyance Li'l Jay knew something they didn't.

"No, Li'l Jay." Margaret kissed him. "I'm not sick."

# 6

By Friday the snow had melted and now the gray slate sidewalk was crossed with shadows of brownstones. It had been a week since Maizon and Margaret had spoken. Margaret wouldn't return her phone calls. On the school bus, Margaret spread books on the seat next to her own and made it seem as though she were too busy with schoolwork to talk. But they would have to talk soon. The play was scheduled for the middle of March and they needed to rehearse.

*Home*, Maizon thought to herself, making her way slowly down Madison Street. She sighed. Ms. Dell would say it was something in the air that made everything seem so crazy. "Home," she said out loud. This is not how she remembered it.

A wind, too warm for February, blew her hair across her eyes. It was long now, almost as long as Margaret's, and according to her grandmother, nappy as the day is long. But Maizon liked it this way, tangled and kinking down against her neck. Ms. Dell had offered to pull a hot comb through it, to straighten it out a little, but Maizon had refused. When it was wet, she braided thick plaits all over her head and let it dry this way. Then she brushed it loose and usually pulled it to the back of her head with a black ribbon. Maizon took a deep breath. The air smelled clean, like spring. She hugged herself as she walked, and squinted up into the sun. "Home again, home again, jiggety-jig," she whispered to herself, remembering the way Grandma used to make her giggle by saying this phrase over and over as she pulled on Maizon's toes.

Maizon let herself into her house and shook herself out of her coat.

"That you, Maizon?" Grandma called from the living room.

"Who else?" Maizon answered back.

"Come in here. I want you to meet somebody."

Maizon made her way to the kitchen first and grabbed a handful of peanuts from the dish on the counter. She had a quick image of Margaret leaning over the toilet making herself throw up and put some of the peanuts back. They had never gone this long without talking before. Maizon couldn't help feeling like she had come home to a Margaret she no longer knew. Before, she could talk to Margaret about anything. Now, it seemed they were so careful around each other; like they had to think a whole lot about something before they said it.

On her way into the living room Maizon passed a huge duffel bag leaning against the dining-room wall. She heard a man's voice, smooth and even, then her grandmother's voice, rising above it. Maizon closed her hand over the peanuts nervously and stepped into the living room.

The man sitting on the couch across from her Grandma's chair seemed familiar. He was tall and brown-skinned with black hair that looked as though it had been sprinkled with salt.

"Hi, Grandma," Maizon said, unable to take her eyes off the man. He sat with his legs crossed at the knee, swishing a cup of something between his hands. He seemed fidgety.

"Maizon?" His voice was hoarse and deep. Maizon took a step back without thinking and looked at Grandma.

"Maizon . . ." Grandma began slowly. "This is your—"

"I know," Maizon said softly.

He had left her at Grandma's when she was a baby, but she would know him—in a hundred thousand people she would know her father even though she had only seen pictures. He smiled at Maizon now, but Maizon couldn't fix her mouth to smile back. They were suspended for a moment; him smiling uncertainly, Grandma looking on with no expression, and Maizon with her mouth partially open, unable to take her eyes off him.

He took a deep breath. "You've grown up," he said, letting go of a proud laugh. "Look at you." He leaned toward Maizon and she stepped back even farther. Just as quickly as his laugh had come, it was gone. He leaned back again, a hurt look moving up into his eyes. "I want to tell you things, Maizon. . . ." His voice broke on her name. "We have a lot to talk about."

Maizon shook her head. She wanted to touch him, to

see if she could feel any realness there. This was a dream, she thought. A dream, a dream. She swallowed and moved closer to Grandma.

"Maizon . . ." Grandma pulled Maizon to her. "Cooper wanted to see you. He's come a long way. . . ."

Cooper. Cooper Devalle Thompson. There was a time, before Grandma adopted her, when she had been Maizon Thompson. There had been a time before all of this when she had been somebody else's child beside Grandma's. When she had belonged to Cooper Devalle Thompson. Such a beautiful name. She let it move over and over in her mind. Still, standing there, Maizon couldn't bring herself to say the name out loud. She had never said it out loud. She had never called anybody Cooper Devalle Thompson. She had never called anybody "Daddy."

"How far did you come?" she asked him now, unable to break her gaze from his eyes. They were so like her own: brown, slanted, with dark heavy lashes.

Cooper looked thoughtful, his thick brows wrinkling across his forehead. "Was in California for a time. Then Seattle. Went up to Vancouver for a while." His voice was deep and flat, uninflected. Maizon wanted there to be more life to it. She had imagined he'd be so full of life. She had imagined a TV dad who would bound into a room and swoop her up into the air. That was a long time ago.

"California's three thousand miles away. The only way it'd take you this long to get from there to here is if you walked," Maizon said. "Real slowly." Her own voice sounded unfamiliar. She was suprised at how controlled it was. "Did you walk?"

Cooper looked down into his cup. He was grinning. Maizon's stomach dipped. If someone had said this to her, she would have grinned too. "Didn't walk," he said. "Hear you've been doing some traveling yourself—"

"You left me with Grandma after Mama died," Maizon cut him off. "Mama died having me. She died at the hospital and they gave you the baby and you gave the baby to Grandma. I'm hers. I don't have anything to do with you. I don't know you. I don't want to know you."

Cooper was staring at her now, his eyes filling quickly. Maizon had never seen a man cry. There was a knot in her stomach like a tiny ball of hate. But when she saw his eyes fill, she felt the knot melting a little. She couldn't get over his eyes. It was as though she were looking into a mirror and seeing her own eyes in somebody else's face.

"You can't have me back," she said.

"Maizon . . ." Grandma began.

Maizon took a step away from them and glared at Grandma. "I don't care. I don't want him in my life." She turned back to Cooper. "You missed it. You missed my whole life!" She was yelling now, her voice filling the large living room. "My life is over now and you missed it. You missed everything."

She remembered the peanuts, growing sweaty in her hand. She didn't want him to have her eyes. "I don't want you in my life! Why'd you come back anyway?"

"Maizon . . ." he was saying, but Maizon wasn't listening. She was raising her hand in the air and flinging the peanuts. Aiming for those eyes. Then she was backing up and running, back through the kitchen, past the long hallway, and out the front door. Then she was running again, as hard as she could, her breath burning in the back of her throat. Running down Madison Street, past it, farther and farther, taking the streets without looking for cars. She couldn't stop. As long as her feet kept propelling her, she wouldn't stop. She wanted to get far away. As far away as she could.

At the corner of Irving and Decatur, Maizon stopped, gulping for breath. It had started raining again, hard cold drops that made her realize she had left the house without a coat. She shivered and sniffed. It had gotten cold suddenly. Very cold—as though Cooper himself had blown in on an icy chill. She wrapped her arms around herself, coughing up sobs. Tears skirted her cheeks, mingling with rain. Maizon couldn't remember feeling this lost before. *I won't let him take me away*, she thought to herself, staring out onto Irving Avenue. There were no cars and the neighborhood seemed deadly silent, as though it was waiting for something to happen.

# 7

"Maizon gone!" Li'l Jay said, running into the room. Margaret glared at him. "Yeah, she's gone home. I just got off of the school bus with her. And you're gone too." She took his hand and led him downstairs. Ms. Dell opened the door and smiled.

"Gone," Li'l Jay said.

"Can you watch him while I get some work done?"

Ms. Dell took Li'l Jay in her arms and pressed his cheek against hers. "I was just thinking about him. Just thinking I'd like some company."

Margaret kissed them both and bounded upstairs

again, locking the door behind her before going to stand in front of the full-length mirror.

Scowling, she turned from side to side. Nothing had changed in the week since she had started her diet. She had read somewhere that a body could exist on grapefruit and water for weeks at a time and had eaten them for a week. There were still a couple of grapefruits stuffed in her dresser drawer, but the thought of having to eat even a tiny piece of another one made her sick now.

"Yuck!" She pulled the baggy sweater up and stared at her stomach. Above it the biggest bra Mama had bought her seemed to be stretching to its limit. "Go away!" she whispered.

"Margaret!"

Margaret jumped. She had not expected Mama to be home this early. On her way upstairs she had checked for the secondhand car Mama had bought right before Christmas. It hadn't been parked on the block, which usually meant Mama wasn't in the neighborhood.

"Coming!" she called, yanking the sweater down.

"Hey, girl!" Mama smiled, kissing Margaret on the

cheek. Margaret was relieved. Mama only greeted her with a "Hey, girl," when she was in a good mood.

Mama set two heavy-looking shopping bags on the table before taking off her coat. "Did a little food shopping after work. Figured I'd get to paint tomorrow," she said, going to the living-room closet. "Li'l Jay downstairs?"

"Yes," Margaret said, feeling stupid. Of course the car having been gone had meant Mama was close by. She only took it for short trips like food shopping during the week. "Ms. Dell wanted some company," she said, staring cautiously at the bags.

"How come you didn't go with him?"

"Had some homework and stuff."

Mama raised her eyebrows. "You're doing homework on a Friday?"

"Figured I'd get it over with."

"Well, don't just sit there looking, Margaret. Help me unpack this stuff." Mama began taking the food out of the bag. "Got these cupcakes you and Li'l Jay like. Figured I'd make tacos for dinner."

Margaret eyed each item Mama handed her to be put

away. Everything seemed to be so fattening. She carried a half gallon of ice cream and a container of milk over to the refrigerator.

"How was your day?" Mama asked, bending beside her to place a container of orange juice in the refrigerator. "Wait a minute! How come this turkey is still here?"

Margaret glanced at slices of turkey wrapped in plastic. She couldn't think of an answer. She had meant to throw the turkey away before Mama saw it. "I took something . . . else for lunch today." She ducked past Mama and headed back for the groceries.

Mama turned. "What?"

"Huh?"

"What did you take, Margaret?" Mama's voice was firm.

"Grapefruit," Margaret mumbled.

"What else?"

Margaret didn't want to lie. She hardly ever lied. But she didn't want Mama to be mad either.

Mama came and stood in front of her, her arms folded. Margaret stared at her feet. "Nothing," she said softly.

Gently, Mama raised Margaret's chin, forcing Margaret to look her in the eye. They had always been close, but now, looking up at her, Margaret saw the confusion in Mama's eyes. A confusion that hadn't been there before. Margaret reached for a bunch of celery, but Mama caught her arm and stopped her. "Think we need to talk," she said, putting an arm across Margaret's shoulders and guiding her into the living room.

"Sit down," Mama said. Margaret sat down on the edge of the couch. Mama sat down beside her.

"What's going on, Margaret?" she asked softly. A tiny crease ran across her forehead. Margaret stared at it to avoid looking her in the eye.

"Nothing. I just wanted grapefruit. Can't I take grapefruit for lunch without everybody going crazy?"

"Everybody's not going crazy, Margaret. Just me. I'm your mother and I have a right to go crazy when I think something's not right with my child. Understand?"

Margaret nodded.

"This isn't the first time I've noticed food I planned for you to eat left in the refrigerator. I figured I'd ignore it and see if you started eating."

"I eat at Ms. Dell's."

"And throw it up," Mama said.

Margaret sat upright. How did Mama know that? How else? That bigmouthed Li'l Jay.

"I wasn't feeling well."

"Margaret." Mama took both Margaret's hands in her own. "I know you're worried about your body growing too quickly. I see the way you're walking and covering yourself up."

*God*, Margaret thought, *are there any secrets around here?*

"I'm getting fat."

Mama squeezed her hands. "Do you think I'm fat?"

Margaret shook her head. "Of course not. You're perfect."

Mama pulled a photo album from beneath the coffee table and flipped through it.

"Remember her?"

Margaret nodded, staring at the picture of Mama. She must have been twelve or thirteen, but already her body seemed to be spreading in every direction.

"My body did the same thing yours is doing. But I caught up to it."

"What if I don't catch up, Mama? What if I look like

Ms. Dell or that big woman down the block? I just don't want to be . . . fat, Mama. . . ."

"You won't get fat, with as much running around as you and Maizon used to do. Why don't you join a team at school—"

"I can't play sports," Margaret said. "Maizon's the athlete. I'm just spastic."

"Why don't you run, then? Just do a couple of laps around the park?"

"I don't even have running shoes."

"I'll buy you running shoes."

"I need a running outfit," Margaret said quickly. "I can't run looking corny."

Mama smiled. "Okay, if I buy you a running outfit, will you promise me you'll run instead of doing this crazy stuff with your diet?"

Margaret was hesitant. "I'll . . . try."

Mama looked stern all of a sudden. "Tonight we're going to sit down and have a normal healthy meal—you, me, and Jay. I want you to eat everything I put in front of you. You understand?"

"Yes," Margaret said.

"Saturday, we'll go shopping for your running outfit."
She took Margaret's face in her hands again. "God, you're
so beautiful. I wish you could see how beautiful you are."

"You're my mother, of course you're going to say that."

Mama smiled and shook her head. "You're not fat."
Her eyes, behind the glasses she had just started wearing,
were sadder than Margaret ever remembered.

"I'm just going to diet for a little while, Mama. Just
until—"

"You're not dieting!"

"You just want me to be fat! You don't care! Ever since
Daddy died, you don't care about anything but yourself!"

Mama was silent, her face flat and empty. Then, slowly,
she shook her head. "I love you, Margaret." Her voice was
small and pained, as though someone had punched her.

# 8

They had been searching for a half hour before they found her, huddled underneath the awning of Ocasio's Grocery Store.

"Maizon!" Margaret called, running from the car with Maizon's coat. "You're all wet." She draped the coat over Maizon's shoulders. "Are you crazy?"

"Who's in there?" Maizon asked, eyeing the car suspiciously.

"Your grandma and Mama."

Maizon didn't move. "I don't want to go back home. Did you meet him?"

Margaret nodded. "He seems nice."

When Margaret and Mama had gone to Grandma's, Margaret couldn't believe her eyes. Mr. Thompson looked so much like Maizon, it was eerie. Her heart dipped when Grandma told her who he was.

"I'm not going back," Maizon said. "I want him to leave."

Margaret looked nervously toward the car. Mama and Grandma were watching them. "You should give him a chance, Maizon."

Maizon eyed her. "Why?"

"Because you have a father," Margaret said. "I'd give anything to have my daddy back."

Maizon sighed, pulling the coat closer to her. Cold rain still blew hard around them. "He can't just leave and come back again. You don't do that."

Margaret nodded. "He could've never come back."

"Yeah, right. I wish. He probably thinks I'm famous or rich or something. He probably heard I was a movie star."

Margaret giggled. "He probably thought he saw you getting an Academy Award."

Maizon let a small smile crease the corners of her mouth. "He probably read somewhere that I got a Nobel Peace Prize."

"Boy, is he going to be disappointed."

Then they were laughing, and with her arm draped over Maizon's shoulder, Margaret led her back to the car.

"Sorry," Maizon mumbled to Grandma, leaning to kiss her on the cheek.

"You had me so worried, Maizon!" In the backseat Grandma pulled Maizon close to her, cradling her head.

"I don't like to be surprised like that," Maizon said.

"And you think I do?" Grandma laughed. "When I opened the door to Cooper, someone could have blown me over with a weak breath."

"Shouldn't have opened the door," Maizon mumbled.

Grandma squeezed her shoulders. "He just wants to get to know you, Maizon."

Maizon sat up. "And then what? He goes away again?"

"If you want him to," Grandma said.

Maizon stared out of the window and sighed. "I don't know what I want."

In the rearview mirror, Mrs. Tory caught Maizon's eye and winked. "Does anybody?"

# 9

Care to join us?" Ms. Dell asked. She and Hattie were sitting in lawn chairs at the top of the stoop. Li'l Jay, bundled in a snowsuit, was playing with a doll at their feet, twisting the head around and around.

"It's not the season," Maizon said.

"It's freezing out," Margaret said, pulling her books closer to her chest.

Ms. Dell laughed. "A little cool air never hurt anyone."

Margaret sat down next to Li'l Jay. Maizon shrugged and sat down beside her.

"Wasn't hard to talk you into it," Hattie smiled. She handed over a thermos. "Hot chocolate."

Maizon took a swallow and held the thermos out for Margaret.

Margaret eyed it. "No, thanks."

"Drink it!" Li'l Jay demanded.

"Shut up," Margaret scolded. But she took the thermos from Hattie and took a small swallow of hot chocolate before handing it back.

"Good girl." Li'l Jay smiled. Margaret stuck her tongue out at him. He was a pain but she loved him. She couldn't help it.

"So what you two know good? That handsome Cooper still around, Maizon?"

Maizon eyed Hattie. They had never really liked each other. Ms. Dell had said it was because they were too much alike, but Maizon couldn't see it. Hattie was a little too man crazy for her liking. "Cooper is too old for you."

Hattie smirked, raising her eyebrows. A long time ago, Margaret and Maizon had agreed that Hattie had the saddest eyes of anyone they'd ever met. But lately Hattie had a way of making her eyes light up. Most of the time when you looked at her now, the sadness was nowhere to be found.

"Are you a one-girl matchmaker?"

Ms. Dell and Margaret laughed.

"He's around," Maizon said, then stared out over the block. When the wind wasn't blowing, it wasn't so cold after all.

"Any idea how long he's staying?"

Maizon shrugged. Cooper had been here a week and a half. Grandma had given him the room down the hall from Maizon's. The room had been Grandma's sewing room for a long time, but now Cooper had moved the sewing machine and all of Grandma's sewing stuff to the basement and had brought a bed and dresser upstairs. Those two items had been down there so long, Maizon didn't even know who they belonged to. Reluctantly, Maizon admitted to herself that Cooper was a good cook. Although dinner was often awkward, filled with too much silence, Grandma seemed to be happy that Cooper was back and Maizon couldn't help letting a little bit of the happiness rub off. Cooper always had a joke for the dinner table, and that seemed to help get rid of some of the tension.

It was strange having a man around the house. He was always fixing something: "That chair could use another nail, don't you think?" and Maizon would nod, even though she had not really noticed the way the chair wobbled until it was fixed. A week and a half, and still she couldn't get used to the idea that this man was her father.

"You still getting those good grades, Maizon?" Cooper had asked yesterday.

"Yes."

Cooper had looked lost for a moment, as though he wanted her to volunteer more information, give them something to talk about.

"That's good," he said.

*We're strangers*, Maizon realized. Even though they shared the same blood, had the same eyes, they were strangers.

"You have your mother's hair, you know?" Cooper had said, eyeing Maizon's braids.

"Grandma told me I did."

"It's nice." Cooper stood with his hands in his pockets, rocking from foot to foot like a little boy. "Guess I'll go get some air. You want to walk?"

"No, thank you. It's too cold."

"Well, then. I guess I'll see you in a bit."

"See you later, Cooper."

It was not supposed to be like this. This isn't how it had been when Maizon imagined him coming back. They would hug for a long time then Cooper would tell her about her mother and his mother and where he had been. He would give her presents and take her around to his friends, saying, "This is my daughter, Maizon, I've been telling you about." They would walk down the block holding hands and everyone would say, "There's Maizon and her dad."

"How's your grandma getting on?" Ms. Dell asked now, interrupting Maizon's thoughts.

Maizon smiled. "Beat her at checkers four times last night. She's waiting for a rematch." Now, like always, Grandma was being patient, giving Maizon and Cooper space, she had said, to get to know each other. "You have to give him a chance," Grandma had said to Maizon over checkers. "Everybody deserves a chance."

Maizon moved closer to Margaret and put her arm around Margaret's shoulders. "What do you think?"

"About what?" Margaret asked.

Maizon shrugged. "You know. About everything?"

A garbage truck barreled noisily past. Li'l Jay waved and two garbagemen waved back.

"Garbagemen coming three times a week now," Ms. Dell said thoughtfully.

Margaret eyed the truck as it turned the corner, heading toward Palmetto Street. The landlord had posted a sign saying he would be increasing everyone's rent by twenty dollars a month. Mama had been relieved that that was all it would be increased, but Ms. Dell and Hattie would have to scrape for it, with Hattie in school and Ms. Dell living off Social Security. Margaret wished again she had twenty dollars to give them every month.

"We'll get by," Ms. Dell said, and Margaret jumped.

Ms. Dell grinned. "Sorry. Your thoughts were coming on pretty strong there for a moment."

Margaret reached up and grabbed the hand Maizon had draped across her shoulders. "I think you should give Cooper a chance. He seems nice. Did you ask him why he left you?"

Maizon picked up a pebble and pitched it into the street. "He said he had been scared. Said he didn't know the first thing about raising a little girl."

"Wouldn't you have been scared, Maiz?"

"Yeah. I guess. Babies freak me a little anyway . . . all tiny and helpless."

"Then you should believe him."

"I'd believe anything that man said to me with his fine self." Hattie laughed.

Maizon rose. "I just had the most horrid thought. What if Hattie and Cooper got married and Hattie became my mom?"

Margaret and Ms. Dell laughed.

"I'd tear into you like Forty Going North," Hattie said. "You could use a good spanking."

Maizon slapped her cheek lightly. "I'd rather eat raw meat than be related to you."

"I'd rather eat a live cow," Hattie said.

They went back and forth for a while before Margaret realized something. Over the months, Hattie and Maizon's cold war had dissolved into a friendly dislike of each other. They sat close to each other now and even, on occasion, touched. Margaret shook her head. Ms. Dell had been right. They were a lot alike and would probably be pretty miserable if each didn't have the other in her life.

# 10

"Cooper?" Maizon said, sitting across from him at the kitchen table. It had been a week since she had talked to Margaret about her father. She had been thinking. Maybe Margaret was right. Maybe all Cooper deserved, all anybody deserved, was a chance.

Cooper was working a phone jack, his hands busy twisting the colored wires. When Maizon called his name, he stopped and looked up at her, all eyes and ears as though he had been put on this earth to listen to her. Maizon felt her stomach flutter. *My* father, she thought. *That man's my father.*

"Are you going to come to my play?"

Cooper nodded. "If you want me to." He stared at her so long, Maizon felt uncomfortable. "I just want to look at you sometimes, Maizon. Sometimes, I can't believe you're real, my daughter, my Maizon."

Maizon swallowed. "I'm nobody's," she said.

"Of course you aren't. Nobody's but your own." Cooper clasped his hands on the table.

"What have you been doing, Cooper? All those years you were gone away when you didn't even write or call to see if I was still alive?"

Cooper was thoughtful. "I was looking for something. I was walking this world trying to figure out who I was in it. I was trying to forget you existed."

Maizon felt herself growing angry. She pressed her hands together under the table and looked Cooper in the eye. "How could you want to forget me?"

She saw the muscles jump in Cooper's neck. Ms. Dell had said that's where men show their pain. She had said, never trust a man in a turtleneck. But Cooper was wearing an oxford shirt, open at the neck. A white oxford shirt, khaki pants, and penny loafers with no socks.

"Sometimes," Cooper said softly, "you have to try to

forget people you love just so you can keep living. Some days I would think of you and all of a sudden, the day would stop and I couldn't do anything but sit and remember the baby you were and remember your mama. I'd get all caught up in the sadness." He shook his head. "I'd just sit there crying for hours and hours and hours." Cooper swallowed and stared down at the table. "I couldn't hold on to jobs. Would get a teaching job one week and the next I'd have a thought of you and your mama and I wouldn't show up for work for days at a time. Couldn't tell them I was sick. And how do you explain to somebody who you're trying to appear stable in front of that you've been grieving for over twelve years?"

When Cooper looked up, his eyes were wet and dark. Maizon turned away from him, feeling her own eyes fill up.

"Why didn't you come home, then?"

"I wanted to. I just wasn't ready."

"I don't know if I'm ready for you to come home now, Cooper."

"I know," Cooper said, his voice breaking. "I know."

# 11

The bridge," Li'l Jay said. He had pulled a chair over to the living-room window and now stood on top of it, his face pressed against the pane.

Margaret sat on the window ledge beside him. In the distance the Williamsburg Bridge loomed brightly out of the darkness.

"You think I'm fat, Li'l Jay?" Margaret asked.

Li'l Jay smiled at her, his dimples like half moons on either side of his face. "No!"

"Would you lie to me, little brother?" Margaret said, poking him in the ribs.

Li'l Jay squealed. "No! No! No!"

Margaret sighed. Mama had taken her to Dr. Nieves a week ago. He swore she was the right weight for her age. He had said she was healthy and alert and had better keep eating if she wanted to stay that way. Mama had told him about the grapefruit diet.

"No grapefruits," Dr. Nieves said, his eyes serious behind the wire-rimmed glasses he wore. He had been her doctor since she was small. "Those fad diets aren't healthy."

Margaret had nodded, remembering how sick she'd felt after eating only grapefruits for a couple of days.

On the way home they stopped at the sporting goods store. Margaret got a pair of Saucony running shoes and a blue-and-red running suit.

Mama walked with her arm around Margaret's shoulders. "I don't want to lose you, Margaret," she had said, her voice low and hollow as though she were holding back tears.

"You won't lose me, Mama," Margaret said.

"I will if you don't eat."

"I'll eat," Margaret promised. A picture of Li'l Jay and her mom alone came into her mind. She swallowed. "I'll eat," she said again, this time really meaning it.

"Here comes a train," Li'l Jay said now. Margaret peered at the bridge.

"I don't see anything," she said, but just as she finished speaking, she heard the train's low whistle. A moment later the train, a dark shadow against the bridge's lights, made its way slowly across. Margaret smiled.

"What do you know, Li'l Jay?" she asked.

Li'l Jay looked at her, his dark eyes bright. "Nothing!"

"Yes, you do. You know what's going to happen, don't you?" Margaret teased. "You probably know what the next million years are going to be like."

Li'l Jay pressed a finger to the window. Margaret stared at it. She remembered the first day Mama and Dad had come home from the hospital with him, a tiny bundle of brown swaddled in white blankets. Jason Tory, Jr. Named for her father. Li'l Jay. She wondered if he'd ever stop being Li'l Jay.

"Maizon has a daddy," Li'l Jay said.

Margaret was silent for a moment. Li'l Jay had said this as though he were asking how come they didn't. "We have a daddy, too, Li'l Jay," she said softly.

Li'l Jay looked up at her. "Where?"

"Up there," Margaret said, pointing past the window at the dark sky. "Heaven."

"Him not coming home?"

Margaret shook her head. "No," she said. "He has a new home. But he watches us."

Li'l Jay stared at her, wide eyed. "Every day?"

"Every day," Margaret said.

Li'l Jay touched her nose with his finger. "You better be good!"

Margaret laughed. "*You* better be good."

# 12

You have to have a little more feeling when you're walking and talking, Caroline," Margaret said, sitting across from her. This was the last rehearsal before the play, and Maizon had skipped out early to go see a movie with Cooper. "I mean, think about it. Here you are, walking home from somewhere the same way you always have, and all of a sudden your route isn't familiar."

"I get it," Caroline said, tossing her hair out of her eyes and beginning again. "The Macons live there," she said, and pointed over her left shoulder. "So I must live here." Caroline took two more steps and looked up. "But I don't." She looked over at Margaret.

Margaret was holding the script and nodding. "That's a lot better. Now the line."

Caroline's voice dropped to a whisper. "Where there once was, there isn't now."

"What there once was, there isn't now," she said again.

Margaret smiled. "That was cool. The best I've seen it."

Caroline blushed. "Something happened. I remembered myself in this neighborhood when I first moved here. And it—it took over, how alone I felt."

"Did you have a lot of friends where you were before?" Margaret asked.

"Yeah. I guess. I had my best friend. We were like you and Maizon. Then I had other friends. I was so scared to move here. Especially when we looked at this apartment and then I checked out the neighborhood—"

"—and saw there weren't any other white girls," Margaret finished.

Caroline nodded. "That was pretty scary."

"Why'd your family move here?"

"It was cheap and my parents want me to grow up around all different kinds of people. Stuff like that. I was thinking about that when I said that line. And that's why it came out sounding different. And you're a good director."

Margaret leaned back on Caroline's couch, her back against the mirror covering the wall behind her. Caroline sat down beside her with a bowl of grapes. "Want some?"

Margaret shook her head. "I had a big dinner before I came over."

Caroline smiled and tilted her head. Over the past months Margaret had begun to like her more and more. She had an easy spirit that seemed to allow her to roll with things. That spirit, Margaret figured, must have been what had gotten her through the first year in the neighborhood.

"I'm glad of two things," Caroline said. "I'm glad you said hello to me on the school bus that first day. I thought I'd be alone for the rest of my life. And I'm glad Maizon asked me to do the monologue." She shoved a handful of grapes into her mouth and chewed for a moment. "It sort of makes sense to me. I mean, she's talking about more than just getting lost. Here is this girl who walks home the same way, day after day after day."

Margaret nodded.

"Then one day, there is not that way to walk home. It reminds me of moving here. All the things that were familiar in my old neighborhood, that I took for granted, just stopped . . . being."

Margaret smiled. Caroline had gotten it. Her interpretation of the monologue was probably different from Maizon's, even from her own, but it sort of got to the same point somehow. The monologue was about "change" and how it affects this one girl. But Margaret realized change affected everybody.

"I like it here now," Caroline said. "I like you and Maizon and Pace."

Margaret was thoughtful. "Sometimes it's hard. There's all this stuff. Maizon doesn't trust white people so much. I think she really likes you sometimes. . . ."

Caroline nodded. "I know not all the time. She's a little moody."

"Yeah. But that's not about you. At that boarding school she kind of had a hard time. And you know Bo?"

"I've heard of him. I think I've seen him."

"You'll meet him at the play. He goes to Baldwin Prep and he's real unkeen about white people. Sometimes I feel all divided."

"People should just like you for who you are," Caroline

said. "They shouldn't judge you by the other people they met who don't even have anything to do with you."

"But sometimes they judge you anyway. It sucks."

"Yeah," Caroline said. "It really does." She crossed her legs in front of her and looked around the living room. "People don't trust each other immediately. My mom says it takes time. Guess I'll have to stick around a bit. Wait it out."

"At least stick around until tomorrow night . . . when you debut."

Caroline giggled. "Who'd've thought it? Me, Caroline Berg. A star."

# 13

A light rain had begun falling by the time Cooper and Maizon emerged from the movie theater. Maizon pulled the hood of her raincoat over head.

"What'd you think?" Cooper asked, putting his arm around Maizon's shoulders. His arm felt warm but unfamiliar. She wasn't sure if she liked it there.

"It was good," Maizon said.

"Some strong storytelling," Cooper said.

The movie had been about five generations of a black family living on an island off the coast of South Carolina. Images of their beautiful clothes and the different ways the women wore their hair zigzagged through Maizon's head now.

"Really good," she said again.

"Want to stop for a milkshake or something?"

Maizon yawned. "I'm kind of tired. Plus, I got school tomorrow and the play." She couldn't help noticing how Cooper's face fell when she said this. In the past few weeks he had been trying really hard to get close to her. But what if they got close and he turned around and left again?

"Guess you're right," Cooper said. "Guess I'll start job-hunting tomorrow. Look around for a place to live.

Maizon's stomach jumped. "Where?"

Cooper laughed. "Where will I look for a job or where will I live?"

Maizon looked at him and felt a sense of pride rush through her. Hattie was right. He was handsome. "Both."

"I'm going to try to get a job over at Baldwin. Got this teaching degree under my belt. Figure that'd be a nice place to work."

"My friend Bo goes there. He says it helps his self-esteem."

Cooper nodded. "That's why it's there. It's a different kind of school, you know."

"Bo says being a black man in the world is harder than anything else. But how does he know? He's just a teenager. And what about black girls?"

Cooper bit his bottom lip. "You start learning early how the world hates you. Somehow I think it's harder for men. I might be wrong, though. But black men aren't just hated, people are afraid of them too. I think that starts making them feel like they're monsters."

"But those boys are all segregated over there."

"A lot of people believe that's what they need right now—support right from the start. Later on, when they go out into the world, they'll feel good about themselves. They'll feel strong."

"How come they don't feel good now?" Maizon shook her head. "I don't get it."

"It's this," Cooper said slowly. "So many times when you open up a newspaper or turn on the television, you see a black man having committed a crime or something else negative. You start associating those images with all black men. . . ."

"That's sometimes how I feel about white people—every time I see a commercial or television show and there aren't any blacks around. Or when I look at a magazine and all the models are white, I start thinking that they make me feel like *I'm* the ugly one. Then I start hating all of them."

"No hate is justified," Cooper said. His voice wasn't angry, but there was a sternness to it that Maizon wasn't sure she appreciated. "But it's what the world does to people. It makes some of us feel ugly and it makes some of us look like criminals, like angry fools. It seems this country picked black men to do the last part to. That's why Baldwin is so important. I wish there was a school like Baldwin Prep for black girls. Maybe it'll happen." Cooper was silent for a moment. When he started speaking again, his voice was softer, wistful. "I wish there had been a school like Baldwin when *I* was growing up. Maybe I wouldn't have run off and left you, afraid of all the responsibility I thought lay ahead of me." He sighed. "Some things you don't know."

Maizon listened. After a moment she realized she was barely breathing. She had gotten caught up in Cooper's speech and couldn't help but feel how angry he was beneath his words. It was a little bit scary, but she wasn't afraid. The anger seemed to make him bigger. It made her feel good, protected, like there was someone strong in the world, looking out for her. She smiled and squeezed Cooper's hand.

"This Bo guy. Is he your boyfriend?"

Maizon felt the heat rise to her face. "No. My friend. I don't have a boyfriend."

"Why not?" Cooper teased.

"'Cause I don't want one," Maizon said. "Got better things to think about."

"Like what?"

"Like my play tomorrow. Are you still going to come?"

Cooper nodded. "That's if you want me to." After a moment he said, "You know that was one of your mama's dreams—to be a writer."

Maizon swallowed. Her mama. "What were some of her other dreams?" she whispered. She wanted to know everything about her mama. Grandma had told her everything she knew. Now it was Cooper's turn.

Cooper slowed down. The rain had faded into a cold mist against their faces. Every now and then a car, its lights bright, moved slowly down the street. Otherwise, the neighborhood was quiet.

"She was beautiful," Cooper said, his voice catching. "Every time I remember her, I remember how beautiful she was. You know"—he looked down at Maizon—"when you first walked in that day I got to your grandma's, I thought I was gonna drop into a dead faint the way you looked so like her."

"Grandma says I do too."

"You and your grandma pretty close, huh?"

Maizon nodded. She couldn't remember a time when Grandma wasn't in her thoughts. If someone had asked who you loved most in your whole life, it wouldn't take her a second to answer.

"Yeah," Cooper said. "I can see that. It's nice."

"Why'd you leave?" Maizon asked suddenly. "Why didn't you stay at Grandma's?"

Cooper shook his head slowly. "I couldn't," he said. "I was young. I was scared. I had just lost the person I loved most in the world. When I felt that helpless bundle in my arms, I knew I wasn't strong enough to give you what you would need to survive. Your grandma was the only woman that could do that."

"What about your parents?"

"My mother died when I was seventeen. Breast cancer. I never knew my dad."

They walked along without speaking for a few minutes.

"You should've kept in touch," Maizon said.

Cooper stopped. Turning to her, he said, "I should've done a lot of things differently. I'm not perfect. This is me, Cooper Devalle Thompson, starting from scratch."

Maizon nodded. "I always wanted a daddy when I was younger. I used to cry for you. I don't cry for you anymore. I outgrew that."

"I'm not asking you to cry for me, Maizon. Just to give me a chance."

"Later on, when I got older, I used to say if you came back, I'd treat you like you never lived," Maizon said.

"Is that what you want to do, now that you know me?"

Maizon thought for a moment. "No," she said. It wasn't what she wanted at all.

# 14

S it here, Grandma," Maizon said, guiding Grandma to a seat beside Ms. Dell's. The auditorium was filling quickly.

"Hi, Grandma," Margaret said, kissing her on the cheek.

"Hi, Margaret. You ever plan to visit this old lady again?"

Margaret smiled. "Have to check my datebook." She put her arm around Grandma. "See if I have time in the next two years."

Grandma laughed.

"Hail, hail, the gang's all here," Maizon sang, surveying the row. Hattie was sitting between Ms. Dell and Mrs. Tory, who had Li'l Jay in her lap. Bo sat beside Mrs. Tory, looking uncomfortable in his navy-blue suit. Maizon winked at him and he waved.

"Where's Cooper?" Margaret asked.

Maizon shrugged, pretending not to care, but more than once Margaret caught her checking over her shoulder to where two teachers were collecting money at the door. Tonight's performances were a fund-raiser for the school.

Caroline walked up the aisle and almost strolled right past their row. Maizon grabbed her dress tail and pulled her back.

"Hey, guys!" Caroline smiled.

"Hey yourself!" Maizon gestured down the row. "You know everybody, right? The Madison Street contingent."

Caroline nodded and waved to the group. "I'm psyched," she said. "Think we should go in the bathroom and go over everything one more time?"

Margaret rolled her eyes. "I'm sick of that monologue. I've heard it a hundred times."

"Yeah," Maizon agreed. "I'm pretty rehearsed out myself."

"Want to go in the bathroom and gossip then?"

"Okay," Margaret and Maizon said at once, jumping up from their seats.

"Who's that cute guy at the end of the row?" Caroline asked, the minute the bathroom door was closed.

Margaret giggled, then began checking under the stall doors to make sure they were empty.

"I don't know," she said casually. "Just a guy I've kissed a couple of times."

"Wait a second," Maizon said, eyeing Margaret suspiciously. "I heard about one kiss that took place about a year ago."

"Oh," Margaret said, too casually. "Guess I forgot to mention the other ones."

Caroline shrieked. "He's fine!"

"He's okay," Maizon said, curling her lip. "Just Bo."

"Are you guys seeing each other?" Caroline asked.

Margaret shook her head. "Not really. We just hang sometimes."

"And kiss," Maizon added. "Don't forget."

Margaret put her arm around Maizon's shoulders. "And kiss."

Maizon frowned. "Man, I can't believe it. Where was I when all this making out was happening?"

Margaret shrugged. "Somewhere between Madison and Palmetto, I guess."

"Yeah," Maizon said. "I guess I was!"

"You and me, Maizon," Caroline said. "Old maids-to-be."

"Boys are still way corny to me," Maizon confided.

Margaret brushed past her, checking her hair in the mirror. "That's 'cause you haven't kissed one."

"That's 'cause I don't want to." Maizon moved in front of her. She stared at their reflections in the mirror. Caroline peered over Margaret's shoulder. "Look at us," Maizon said.

"Where did we come from?" Caroline laughed. "And how the heck did we end up together here?"

On their way out of the bathroom they bumped into Hattie.

"Hey! Where are you going?" Margaret asked. "It's almost time for the performances."

"Touch up my makeup. The wind just blew a pretty handsome breeze our way." She turned and pointed.

At the end of the aisle Cooper stood, searching the auditorium. Maizon smiled. "See that guy over there, Caroline?" she said. Caroline nodded. "That's my dad."

# 15

"Hey, Maizon," Margaret called, catching up to Maizon two weeks later.

"Hey, Margaret," Maizon said. "Where you coming from?"

"Bo and I went to see a movie and got a slice of pizza on Myrtle Avenue."

Maizon put her hands into the pockets of her jeans. "Oh. You gonna puke it up?"

"I'm not doing that anymore," Margaret said. Maizon seemed distant somehow. Her eyes were blank like they were looking at something they had no interest in, even when they looked at Margaret.

"I can't be your friend if you do that, Margaret."

"I can't be my friend," Margaret said. She took Maizon's hand. "Thanks."

"For what?"

Margaret shrugged. "Just for being there, I guess."

"But we haven't seen each other in two weeks." Aside from in school, they had seen little of each other after the play.

"Doesn't matter," Margaret said.

"Yeah." Maizon held tight to Margaret's hand.

In the past few weeks the temperature had climbed consistently. Now, tiny green buds were sprouting on the tree that stood right in the center of the block, an equal distance between Margaret's house and Maizon's. Today it must have been close to fifty degrees.

Maizon sighed. "Today reminds me of Blue Hill." She stopped in front of the tree and smiled. "Remember we used to called this our 'compromise spot'?"

Margaret looked up at the tree and smiled, a million feelings shooting through her at once. She was thinking about her father—this time two years ago he was still alive;

she was thinking about Maizon and Cooper and Bo and this tree and spring creeping up on them. She was wearing her winter coat, a heavy black wool coat her mother had bought on sale somewhere. Now she pulled her arms out and draped it over her shoulders. Maizon sat down, her back against the tree, and Margaret slid down beside her.

"Seems like such a long time ago." Maizon's voice was wistful.

"Everything seems like a long time ago. How's Cooper?"

Maizon squinted and looked up at the tree. Strips of sun streamed through its branches. She inhaled. "Okay. We've sort of been becoming friends, I guess." She smiled.

Maizon's smile was contagious. Margaret wanted to hug her. It seemed like it had been forever since they were last together.

"I kind of like him," Maizon confided. "I mean, he's okay, for a dad. Isn't that strange?"

"What's so strange?"

Maizon shrugged. "I don't know. It's just that all my life I never really knew him, then one day he pops back into my life and it's like he was there all the time."

Margaret swallowed. "You're lucky, Maizon."

Maizon grabbed her hand. "I know. C'mon," she said, pulling Margaret up.

"C'mon where?"

"I don't know. Let's just go somewhere. Do something. Let's just spend the rest of this day together, the way we used to do."

"No Cooper? No Caroline?" Margaret raised an eyebrow.

"No Cooper. No Caroline," Maizon said. "Just you and I for old times. Hey!" Maizon stopped. "How are you feeling?"

"Okay," Margaret said. "Mama was right. Running helps. My body feels different. It's starting to feel okay. Like it belongs to me. I look at Mama's body and it's nice. If that's what I'm going to look like, then I'm okay."

"For real 'okay' or for fake 'okay'?"

Margaret rolled her eyes. "For real okay. I'm really not puking anymore. Sometimes I want to and I start thinking about how crappy it makes me feel. It can kill you, doing that. I don't want to die." She shrugged. "I don't want to be like those girls who make themselves sick to be skinny. You know what?"

"What?" Maizon asked.

"I don't even want to be skinny. For me, skinny's stupid. Healthy's nice. I chant that every day, like a mantra. I'm really starting to believe it."

"Yes!!!" Maizon yelled. She hugged Margaret. "Yes!!!"

Margaret laughed. "You're still crazy, Maizon. Some things don't change."

"Guess what?" Maizon said. "I'm not really so flat chested anymore."

Margaret laughed. "For real not flat chested or for fake?"

Maizon held up her hand. "Scout's honor it's not tissue."

"You were never a Scout, Maizon."

"Well, I'm being as honest as one."

At the corner they passed a group of boys. "Are you two in love or what?" a skinny boy yelled.

Maizon held up their clasped hands and smirked. "Maybe. It's a free country," she yelled.

"It's a free country," the boys mocked.

"It's a—it's a—it's a free country," Maizon yelled over and over at the top of her lungs.

When she stopped yelling, out of breath, Margaret was laughing so hard, her eyes were blurred with tears. "It's a—it's a—it's a free country!" Margaret screamed, not caring that the boys were staring at them like they were crazy. Not caring that people were pushing their windows open to look down at them. This country was a whole lot of things, but it sure wasn't free, Margaret thought, and knew Maizon was thinking the same thing, how ridiculous a statement "It's a free country" really was, how a long, long time ago they had both believed it and would say, "It's a free country," to anyone who dared say, "Get out of my yard" and "Don't say that" or "Don't stand there."

Suddenly Maizon stopped laughing and placed her right hand over her heart. "I pledge allegiance," she began solemnly.

Margaret jumped into a standing position and did the same thing. "I pledge allegiance," she said.

"To my friend," Maizon continued, looking up at the leaves. The first time she and Margaret had chanted this, they were in the fourth grade and had just realized what the Pledge of Allegiance meant. "Let's pledge allegiance to us," Maizon had suggested.

Margaret raised her head. Streams of sun poured past the branches.

"To my friend," Margaret said.

"And to the United States of Me!" they finished in unison, then looked at each other and smiled.

"Grandma said I should invite you over for waffles tomorrow."

Margaret raised an eyebrow. "With bananas?"

"Blueberries and bananas."

"I think it would be in my best interest to spend the night so that I can be on time," Margaret said, trying to keep a straight face. "First you have to run with me in the morning, though."

Maizon scowled. "I hate running."

"I'll go slow."

"I'll ride my bike."

Margaret thought for a moment, then smiled. "Deal."

Maizon took her hand again, leading her toward Palmetto. "Feel like we've walked this strip a trillion times."

"Trillion and one easily," Margaret said.

Maizon took a deep breath. The air was cool against the back of her throat. "You still kissing all over Bo?"

"Not all over, just on the lips, sometimes."

"Yuck!" Maizon said, making a face. "Spit swapper."

"He actually kisses all right."

Maizon rolled her eyes. "As if you have something to compare it to."

Margaret giggled. "You know something, Maiz?"

"You're going to say this is the happiest you've felt in a long time."

Margaret stopped, raising her eyebrows. "How'd you know that?"

"'Cause it's the happiest I've felt in a long time."

"Honest?"

"Honest!"

"This is what Ms. Dell knew, and probably Li'l Jay," Margaret began wonderingly. "That we would be all right after all. That all this stuff would happen to us, but in the end we'd be okay."

Maizon nodded. "None of them—Ms. Dell, your mom, my grandma, Li'l Jay, even Cooper and Hattie— none of them would ever let anything happen to us, Margaret."

"We're their favorite girls." Margaret laughed.

"We are. I came back from Blue Hill and it was like they were all waiting for me, ready to take me in like a prodigal daughter."

"But you didn't feel like you belonged here then."

Maizon was thoughtful. "I still don't. I mean, I still feel like a part of me is somewhere else—like I live between two worlds."

"You think that feeling's ever going to go away?"

Maizon shook her head. "I doubt it. But it's okay. I feel so good today. And Cooper coming back is like a new beginning to returning to Madison Street. You get what I'm saying?" She looked at Margaret, searching her eyes. Margaret nodded.

"Even you and me walking today," Maizon said. "Us together with nobody else, they way it used to be—this is a new beginning of us the old way."

Maizon smiled in a way that Margaret recognized from a long time ago, before Blue Hill, before her father died, before everything started changing.

"Margaret and Maizon!!" Maizon yelled, waving a fist into the air. "Friends forever!!"

"Yeah," Margaret said, feeling happiness warm her all over. "We're going to be two old ladies together," she said. "Sitting in rocking chairs on my stoop." She linked her fingers into Maizon's.

"Talking about what used to be," Maizon said. "Clicking our false teeth, drinking tea, pulling our shawls up over our shoulders . . ."

"Remembering," Margaret said, squeezing Maizon's hand. "And these two little girls will come up and sit on the stoop and we'll tell them how much they remind us of ourselves at their age."

"And those girls will probably laugh and yell about how they're going to be friends forever."

"They will be," Margaret said, knowing it would happen like this to other girls. Believing it would happen a million and one times more . . . somewhere . . . between Madison and Palmetto.

Turn the page for a look
at **JACQUELINE WOODSON**'s
moving story of her childhood.

**Winner of the National Book Award**

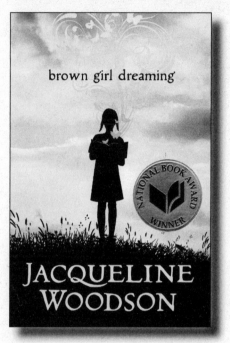

**A *Kirkus Reviews* Best Book of 2014**

"Gorgeous."                    —*Vanity Fair*

"This is a book full of poems that cry out to be
learned by heart. These are poems that will, for
years to come, be stored in our bloodstream."
                    —*The New York Times Book Review*

"Moving and resonant . . . captivating."
                    —*The Wall Street Journal*

"A radiantly warm memoir." —*The Washington Post*

# february 12, 1963

I am born on a Tuesday at University Hospital
Columbus, Ohio,
USA—
a country caught

between Black and White.

I am born not long from the time
or far from the place
where
my great-great-grandparents
worked the deep rich land
unfree
dawn till dusk
unpaid
drank cool water from scooped-out gourds
looked up and followed
the sky's mirrored constellation
to freedom.

I am born as the South explodes,
too many people too many years

enslaved, then emancipated
but not free, the people
who look like me
keep fighting
and marching
and getting killed
so that today—
February 12, 1963
and every day from this moment on,
brown children like me can grow up
free. Can grow up
learning and voting and walking and riding
wherever *we* want.

I am born in Ohio but
the stories of South Carolina already run
like rivers
through my veins.

# second daughter's second day on earth

My birth certificate says: Female Negro
Mother: Mary Anne Irby, 22, Negro
Father: Jack Austin Woodson, 25, Negro

In Birmingham, Alabama, Martin Luther King Jr.
    is planning a march on Washington, where
John F. Kennedy is president.
In Harlem, Malcolm X is standing on a soapbox
    talking about a revolution.

> *Outside the window of University Hospital,*
> *snow is slowly falling. So much already*
> *covers this vast Ohio ground.*

In Montgomery, only seven years have passed
    since Rosa Parks refused
to give up
her seat on a city bus.

> *I am born brown-skinned, black-haired*
> *and wide-eyed.*
> *I am born Negro here and Colored there*

and somewhere else,
the Freedom Singers have linked arms,
their protests rising into song:
*Deep in my heart, I do believe*
*that we shall overcome someday.*

and somewhere else, James Baldwin
is writing about injustice, each novel,
each essay, changing the world.

> *I do not yet know who I'll be*
> *what I'll say*
> *how I'll say it . . .*

Not even three years have passed since a brown girl
named Ruby Bridges
walked into an all-white school.
Armed guards surrounded her while hundreds
of white people spat and called her names.

She was six years old.

> *I do not know if I'll be strong like Ruby.*
> *I do not know what the world will look like*
> *when I am finally able to walk, speak, write . . .*
> Another Buckeye!
> *the nurse says to my mother.*
> *Already, I am being named for this place.*

*Ohio. The Buckeye State.*
*My fingers curl into fists, automatically*
This is the way, *my mother said,*
of every baby's hand.
*I do not know if these hands will become*
*Malcolm's—raised and fisted*
*or Martin's—open and asking*
*or James's—curled around a pen.*
*I do not know if these hands will be*
*Rosa's*
*or Ruby's*
*gently gloved*
*and fiercely folded*
*calmly in a lap,*
*on a desk,*
*around a book,*
*ready*
*to change the world . . .*

# a girl named jack

*Good enough name for me,* my father said
the day I was born.
*Don't see why*
*she can't have it, too.*

But the women said no.
My mother first.
Then each aunt, pulling my pink blanket back
patting the crop of thick curls
tugging at my new toes
touching my cheeks.

*We won't have a girl named Jack,* my mother said.

And my father's sisters whispered,
*A boy named Jack was bad enough.*
But only so my mother could hear.
*Name a girl Jack,* my father said,
*and she can't help but*
*grow up strong.*
*Raise her right,* my father said,
*and she'll make that name her own.*

*Name a girl Jack*
*and people will look at her twice,* my father said.

*For no good reason but to ask if her parents*
*were crazy,* my mother said.

And back and forth it went until I was Jackie
and my father left the hospital mad.

My mother said to my aunts,
*Hand me that pen,* wrote
*Jacqueline* where it asked for a name.
Jacqueline, just in case
someone thought to drop the *ie.*

Jacqueline, just in case
I grew up and wanted something a little bit longer
and further away from
Jack.

# the woodsons of ohio

My father's family
can trace their history back
to Thomas Woodson of Chillicothe, said to be
the first son
of Thomas Jefferson and Sally Hemings
some say
this isn't so but . . .

the Woodsons of Ohio know
what the Woodsons coming before them
left behind, in Bibles, in stories,
in history coming down through time

so

ask any Woodson why
you can't go down the Woodson line
without
finding
doctors and lawyers and teachers
athletes and scholars and people in government
they'll say,

*We had a head start.*
They'll say,
*Thomas Woodson expected the best of us.*
They'll lean back, lace their fingers
across their chests,
smile a smile that's older than time, say,

*Well it all started back before Thomas Jefferson*
*Woodson of Chillicothe . . .*

and they'll begin to tell our long, long story.

# the ghosts of the
# nelsonville house

The Woodsons are one
of the few Black families in this town, their house
is big and white and sits
on a hill.

Look up
to see them
through the high windows
inside a kitchen filled with the light
of a watery Nelsonville sun. In the parlor
a fireplace burns warmth
into the long Ohio winter.

Keep looking and it's spring again,
the light's gold now, and dancing
across the pine floors.

Once, there were so many children here
running through this house
up and down the stairs, hiding under beds
and in trunks,

sneaking into the kitchen for tiny pieces
of icebox cake, cold fried chicken,
thick slices of their mother's honey ham . . .

Once, my father was a baby here
and then he was a boy . . .

But that was a long time ago.

In the photos my grandfather is taller than everybody
and my grandmother just an inch smaller.

On the walls their children run through fields,
    play in pools,
dance in teen-filled rooms, all of them

grown up and gone now—
but wait!

Look closely:

There's Aunt Alicia, the baby girl,
curls spiraling over her shoulders, her hands
cupped around a bouquet of flowers. Only
four years old in that picture, and already,
a reader.

Beside Alicia another picture, my father, Jack,

the oldest boy.
Eight years old and mad about something
or is it someone
we cannot see?

In another picture, my uncle Woody,
baby boy
laughing and pointing
the Nelsonville house behind him and maybe
his brother at the end of his pointed finger.

My aunt Anne in her nurse's uniform,
my aunt Ada in her university sweater
*Buckeye to the bone* . . .

The children of Hope and Grace.

Look closely. There I am
in the furrow of Jack's brow,
in the slyness of Alicia's smile,
in the bend of Grace's hand . . .

There I am . . .

Beginning.

## it'll be scary
## sometimes

My great-great-grandfather on my father's side
was born free in Ohio,

1832.

Built his home and farmed his land,
then dug for coal when the farming
wasn't enough. Fought hard
in the war. His name in stone now
on the Civil War Memorial:

*William J. Woodson*
*United States Colored Troops,*
*Union, Company B 5th Regt.*

A long time dead but living still
among the other soldiers
on that monument in Washington, D.C.

His son was sent to Nelsonville
lived with an aunt

William Woodson
the only brown boy in an all-white school.

*You'll face this in your life someday,*
my mother will tell us
over and over again.
*A moment when you walk into a room and*

*no one there is like you.*

*It'll be scary sometimes. But think of William Woodson*
*and you'll be all right.*

LastSummer with Maizon

JACQUELINE WOODSON
Three-time Newbery Honor Author

"Ms. Woodson writes with a sure understanding of the thoughts of young people, offering a poetic, eloquent narrative that is not simply a story of nearly adolescent children, but a mature exploration of grown-up issues: death, racism, independence, the nurturing of the gifted black child and, most important, self-discovery."
—*The New York Times*

"The best-friendship of two young black girls in Brooklyn is honestly portrayed, including the little swipes of meanness that jostle with the shared care and loyalty to make a bond."
—*The Bulletin of the Center for Children's Books*

MaizonatBlueHill

JACQUELINE WOODSON
Winner of the National Book Award

**An ALA Best Book for Young Adults**

★ "Simply told, this is a finely crafted sequel to
*Last Summer with Maizon.*"
—*Publishers Weekly,* starred review

"Woodson's story frankly confronts issues of color,
class, prejudice, and identity."          —*Booklist*

"A provocative glimpse of the pain and beauty of
a gifted girl's adolescence."
—*School Library Journal*